CONTENTS

ACKNOWLEDGMENTS

Cover design by Jesse Brady. Find more of Jesse's artwork at jessebradyart.com.

THE LEGEND OF BATTLE ISLAND

MATT KORVER

ISBN-9781799118602

CHAPTER ONE

DISCO FEVER

Disco music.

My eyes popped open. Who could be playing loud disco music at — I looked at my alarm clock — 4 a.m.?!

I live in a quiet neighborhood. The type of neighborhood where the mailman knows your name and you know his (Ours is "Dale"). The type of neighborhood where you feel OK asking the guy next door to watch your cat while you're away. The type of neighborhood where old ladies hang "neighborhood watch" signs in their window to let hooligans know that this is a pleasant place, and shenanigans are not welcome.

This neighborhood definitely does not throw disco parties at 4 a.m.

I opened my window to warn the dance party that old Mrs. Donovan was about to call the cops when I saw the strangest thing I'd ever seen. A man in army clothes was dancing wildly in the middle of the street — wait, that's not the strange part — with a disco ball floating over his head — still not the strangest part — and he didn't seem to be enjoying it at all! Now I can't say for sure because I'm not really a dancer, but it seems that if you're the type of person who chooses to dance in public, a 4 a.m. disco party should be the highlight of your life. This guy seemed to be running for his life.

"Hey!" I yelled. "Dancing guy! Are you OK? Is something—"

I stopped in the middle of my sentence when I saw what he was running from. A panda bear was chasing him with a shotgun. Do pandas know how to use shotguns? They don't, right? I feel like I would have heard about that on the news. And even if they did, their paws are much too big to squeeze the…

POW!

The panda ended the dance party with one shot. I gasped and covered my mouth. The army guy didn't stagger around or gush blood or do any of the things you'd expect someone to do when they've been shotgunned. Instead, he just dropped some glowing weapons and disappeared into a weird white light.

I stood there frozen with my hand over my mouth. Why did this have to happen tonight of all nights? For the first time in my life, I was sleeping in an empty house. I'd felt like a real big shot earlier in the week when my parents had left on their anniversary trip, but now I wanted nothing more than to hide under the covers and scream for my mom. I started reaching for my phone so I could do just that, but the panda locked eyes with me before I could grab it.

My heart sank.

This wasn't a real panda bear at all. If it were a real panda, I could have breathed a sigh of relief because murderous, shotgun-toting pandas do not exist, meaning I was in a dream. No, this was scarier than a murderous shotgun-toting panda. It was a murderous shotgun-toting psycho dressed in a panda Halloween costume. I ducked and started crawling. Maybe I could hide under my bed. Maybe he didn't actually see me. Maybe…

KACHUNK! KACHUNK! KACHUNK!

I glanced back out my window and had to hold back a scream. The psycho panda was not only sprinting toward my house, but he was also somehow building a ramp straight to my bedroom!

"NononononoNONONONONONO!"

I got up and ran toward my bedroom door. No time to put on pants — Mrs. Donovan was about to get a nice view of the old P.E. shirt and polka dot boxers I slept in.

Zingzingzing!

Bullets tore through the room. Then, just as I rolled out my bedroom door —

BOOOOOOOOM!

An explosion rocked the house and tossed me to the ground. I curled into a ball and peeked through my fingers just in time to see the panda disappear into the same white light that had taken the army guy. Then the smoke from the explosion cleared, and I saw that my bedroom wall was no more. I leaped to my feet and ran downstairs for the back door. Just as I was about to open the door, however, I heard footsteps outside.

Shuffle shuffle.

I stopped. How many of these guys were there?!

Shuffle shuffle.

I spun against the wall. The footsteps stopped. I tried to quiet my loud breathing. Then I heard a new noise.

Beep. Beep. Beep.

The footsteps ran away, but the beeping continued.

Beep. Beep. Beep.

I waited for a moment, then dared to creep toward my kitchen window. I peeked outside.

Beep.

Looked to my left.

Beep.

Looked to my right.

Beep.

Looked down.

Beep.

That's when I saw it. A small, black explosive stuck to my house.

"AHHHH—"

BOOOOOOOOOOOOOOOOOOM!

That was the first time I ever exploded. I wish I could say it was my last.

CHAPTER TWO

TOMATO HEAD

Party music.

I opened my eyes, looked around, then — OK, so I'm going to tell you what I saw, but first, I feel like I need to warn you. You know how your brain automatically tunes out anytime someone starts talking about their dream? Like, you might really try to pay attention, but then they get to the part where their sister who was actually their grandma gave them a banana that transformed them into Donkey Kong, but maybe it was King Kong, and — see? You started skipping ahead. I'm going to need you to not do that for this next part because it'll sound very much like one of those weird dreams, but I promise, it was 100 percent real.

I was sitting on a bus. I believe it was the bus I used to ride to my elementary school. It was blaring party music. Still following along? Good. I opened the window and peeked down to see if the bus was blue like I remember from my elementary days. It was blue. It was also floating 5,000 feet above the island where I lived. How was it floating? Great question. I'm glad you're still with me. It was floating because it had a hot air balloon strapped to its roof.

I rubbed my eyes and let that sink in. There was really only one option here: I was on the bus to heaven. Give the angels points for creativity, I guess. I sighed. This was not how I'd expected the end of my life to go, but at least I'd lived long enough to see high school. I leaned out the window to wave one last goodbye to my island home, then settled in and smiled at the guy sitting next to me. He was wearing a tomato on his head.

"Hey," I said. "You dead too?"

Tomato Head didn't respond.

"My name's Pete." I stuck out my hand. "Pete Kartson."

Tomato Head didn't shake.

I continued holding out my hand. "I live on that island down there. Well, *lived*, I guess. I just exploded, unfortunately."

Tomato Head looked me in the eye, glanced down, then faced forward without saying a word. I looked down too, then turned red. I was still in my boxers.

"Listen, I—I didn't know I was going to die," I stammered. "I have pants at home, and if I'd had just a few more seconds, I would have..." I stopped. I didn't know why I felt the need to explain myself to someone wearing a tomato on his head.

The guy shook his big head, then walked to the back of the bus to join about 50 other freaks in costumes. There were a bunch of people dressed in army fatigues, a lifeguard, an astronaut, two Vikings, and a guy who looked like Keanu Reeves from that movie where he shoots a zillion people.

"Hey! Excuse me!" Nobody turned around. I got out of my seat. "Is everyone here dead?" When it became clear no one would be answering, I glanced back out the window and squinted. Wait a second. We weren't floating away from the island. We were floating toward it.

Just then, the bus's back door flew open, and Tomato Head jumped out.

"Whoa!" I yelled. "Did he have a parachute?! It didn't look like he had a parachute!"

Nobody listened to me. Twenty more people followed Tomato Head to the ground.

I got so mad at everyone for not listening to me that I stomped to the middle of the aisle and screamed, "WHY IS EVERYONE JUMPING?!"

People from the front of the bus stood up and started walking toward me. But instead of answering my question, they pushed me toward the open door.

"Hey, wait! I don't want to go back there!" I yelled, trying to hang on to the back of a seat. Nobody cared. The growing tide of costumed weirdos pushed until I ran out of things to grab and fell out of the bus.

CHAPTER THREE
BOOGIE BOMB

As I plummeted to my second death that day, I thought about the time my buddy Jackson asked me to go skydiving with him.

"You think I'm going to pay $100 to jump out of a plane?" I'd asked with my mouth hanging open.

"Oh, it was $100 with the Groupon, but that expired. It's $200 now."

"Why would anyone pay that?!"

"Something to do."

"If I'm so bored that I need someone to push me out of a plane because it's 'something to do,' I'm going to need you to shoot me, OK?"

"You know you get a free t-shirt too, right?"

"I'M NOT DOING IT!"

Jackson had shrugged. "You're missing out."

I'd felt a little bad at the time, but now I realized just how wrong Jackson was. Turns out, not falling out of a plane is WAY better than falling out of a plane.

I looked down to see where I was going to splat. Oh, cool. The clock tower. I've always wanted to get impaled on a clock tower.

SHING!

A lifeguard that had been falling below me opened a glider.

"Where did you get that?!" I tried yelling as I fell past her.

SHING! SHING! SHING!

More gliders popped out. A parachute. One of those Chinese New Year dragon things. I felt my back and discovered a backpack that definitely hadn't been there before. I tugged at a strap and — *SHING!* — a glider popped out.

I took a moment to breathe and look down at my island. It was pretty cool to see all the mountains and rivers and towns from way up here. I soaked in the view for a moment, then banked toward my house. Pants time. As I approached my neighborhood, I noticed that I wasn't alone. At least a half dozen other people were landing at Pinecrest Park. I took a deep breath, swooped toward my house, and —

"AHHH!"

A woman with green pigtails dropped in first and started hacking my roof with a giant lollipop. I veered away at the last second and landed in the middle of the street.

OK, no more pants. Time to run and hide.

I sprinted toward Jackson's house. His house had one of those old cellars that seemed safe.

"Pete!" I spun around. Dale the mailman was pointing to my bare legs. "Forgot something, buddy?"

"I'm working on it!"

Dale grinned. "Just giving you a hard time. Hey, do you want to take your mail, or should I put it in your box?"

"Little busy!"

"No problem, I'll try to fit it in the box. It's just that you haven't gotten your mail for the last few days, and there's not much room in there. I know your parents are out of town, but you have to remember to do that."

I frantically looked both ways down the street. "Uh, sorry, I just..."

"No worries," Dale waved his hand. "I know it's easy to forget. Especially with all this going on."

I stopped. "All what? Do you know what's happening?"

CRACK!

Dale disappeared in a flash of light. Behind him stood an astronaut with a shotgun.

I started running and explaining myself at the same time.

"HELLO!" I shouted over my shoulder. "I'M NOT YOUR ENEMY!"

CRACK!

The astronaut shot at me.

"IN FACT, I WOULD SAY THAT I'M A FRIEND OF THE SPACE PROGRAM!"

CRACK!

"WHAT DO YOU THINK ABOUT PUTTING AWAY THE GUN, AND MAYBE WE CAN JUST TALK!"

CRACK!

That time, something hit my shoulder. It didn't hurt like I thought it would — it felt more like a bee sting than anything else. Still, my mind screamed, "YOU JUST GOT SHOT WITH A REAL GUN!" I collapsed and threw my hands in the air to surrender. "Please don't shoot me. Please. I already blew up once today."

CRACK!

"NOOOOOO!" I squeezed my eyes closed and waited for the light to get me, but it never did. I opened my eyes to see the white light sucking up the astronaut instead.

"Grab his gun!"

I spun around. Jackson was running behind me. "Wait, did you shoot him?!" I asked.

"I said grab his gun! We gotta go."

"Did you really just shoot another person?! An astronaut no less!"

"I SAID..."

Rat-tat-tat-tat-tat!

The green-haired girl started firing at us with a machine gun. Jackson protected us by magically building a wall in the same way I'd seen the panda build the ramp the night before. "ARE YOU GOING TO GRAB THE GUN OR NOT?!"

"HOW DID YOU DO THAT?!"

Rat-tat-tat-tat-tat!

Instead of answering, Jackson dove into a nearby gas station. I grabbed the shotgun and ducked behind the counter with him. "OK, she's probably going to come from the north," Jackson said.

"Which way is north?"

Jackson looked at me like I was an idiot.

"I don't know directions! You know that."

"That way. Now, she'll be trying to outflank us, so..."

"What does that mean?"

"Pete, come on!"

"No, you come on! What, did you join the Marines overnight?"

Jackson gave up trying to explain things to me and started talking to himself. "High ground, high ground. Where's the high ground?"

I grabbed Jackson's shoulder. "Stop for one second and focus."

"I'm kind of focused on not getting killed right now."

"I'm not wearing pants."

Jackson glanced down. "I see that."

"Do you know why that is? BECAUSE SOMEONE PUT A BOMB ON MY HOUSE LAST NIGHT!"

"OK. We gotta move."

"Are you listening?! We're hiding here until all the psychos leave, and then we're going back to my house and getting pants!"

Rat-tat-tat-tat-tat!

The green-haired girl started shooting the counter. Jackson jumped up to return fire, then escorted me out the back door. He built another one of his magic ramps up to the gas station's roof, then opened a treasure chest that happened to be up there like it was the most normal thing in the world for gas stations to have treasure chests on their roofs. A few guns popped out as well as a multicolored ball.

I picked up the ball. "What's this?"

Jackson looked over. "I think they call that a boogie bomb."

"A bomb?!" I dropped the ball like it was a hot coal.

Jackson's eyes got big. "Don't..."

BWOW!

As soon as the boogie bomb touched the ground, it exploded in a rainbow flash and started playing disco music. When it did, I felt an overwhelming urge to dance. So right there, with the pigtailed menace standing below, I dropped everything and danced with all my might. "What's going on?!"

I looked over to see that Jackson was dancing just as hard as I was. He even had a little disco ball floating above his head like the army guy I'd seen outside my house. He looked mad at me. "You dope." Just then, Green Pigtails threw a glowing metal thing onto our roof. Jackson nodded at it while continuing to dance. "Grenade."

I tried to pick it up and throw it back. I tried so hard. But I just couldn't stop dan…

BOOM!

I exploded for the second time in my life.

CHAPTER FOUR

PERFECT POTTY ISLAND

I glared at Jackson. The explosion had sent us both back to the floating party bus. "You wanna tell me what's going on now?!"

Jackson sighed. "You forgot to check the mail, didn't you?"

"I've been busy!"

Jackson pulled a letter out of his pocket and plopped it in my lap. The letter was written on the official stationery of Mayor Pierre Parfait.

"Oh no," I said. "Don't tell me this is another one of his dumb money-making schemes."

Jackson nodded.

I looked at the ceiling. Mayor Pierre Parfait was not what you would call a good mayor. It's not like he didn't try — he actually tried so, so hard to be a good mayor for our little island. It's just that he had lots of bad ideas. Like WeaselCon, the first and only international convention for weasel owners. Before the convention even started, every last weasel escaped. Making things worse, the mayor then shipped a bunch of llamas over to the island since he believed that llamas are the natural enemy of the weasel. They are not. Our little island is still teeming with weasels and llamas.

Then there was the time he stunk up the island for weeks when he tried to attract tourists by building the world's largest cheese sculpture. And the time he changed our national anthem to polka to improve album sales for his polka band. And the time he sold our island's naming rights to a local corporation. "Now, wait a second," you might be saying. "That last one doesn't sound so bad!" Actually, it is. The only island business interested in naming rights was the local factory. It's a toilet factory. So now I have to tell people I live on Perfect Potty Island.

I started reading the letter.

Dear residents of Perfect Potty Island,

I hope this letter finds you well. I am excited to

announce that our island has been presented with a unique opportunity from a generous member of our community. Effective at midnight tonight, our fair island will be renamed "Battle Island!" Accompanying this wonderful new name are several other minor changes that you should be aware of.

1. Our island is temporarily being transformed into a "battle royale" battleground (Or, as I like to call it, a *playground*!). For those unfamiliar with the battle royale concept, you are in for a treat! One hundred warriors will descend on Battle Island several times a day to find out who is the strongest. They will fight to the death until one warrior is left. Isn't that exciting?

2. DON'T WORRY! Nobody actually dies! Their weapons look real, but I am told they are not. They use fun, new technology to beam their victims back to a "battle bus."

3. Oh, also, a bus will be floating over the island several times a day. It's actually the Pinecrest Elementary bus. Now that I think about it, we will probably have to cancel school until we find a new bus.

4. Now for the most exciting news: Battle Island residents are invited to participate in the battle royale free of charge! If you are the last person standing, you are eligible for a host of wonderful prizes, including an umbrella.

5. If you do not wish to participate, that is not a problem. You may occasionally run into a battle royale visitor eager to involve you in the game. If this happens to you, you may simply request that they do not shoot you. I am told that our new friends are quite understanding about this.

6. May the odds be ever in your favor!

7. (That is a reference to The Hunger Games, a famous battle royale contest where children try to kill each other.)

Fondly,
Mayor Pierre Parfait

I looked at Jackson when I finished reading the letter. "He's nuts."

"I know," Jackson said. "I don't know why he always signs these things, 'Fondly.'"

"NO! I mean with this whole battle royale thing!"

Jackson shrugged. "I mean it's not great, but if they closed the elementary school, I'll bet they cancel our classes too." He thought about it some more, and his eyes lit up. "And my dad probably won't make me work for him this afternoon either!"

"SOMEONE JUST BLEW US UP!"

"Would you rather get fake exploded or test toilets for three hours?"

"Test toilets. For sure."

Jackson cocked his head. "You say that, but that's just because you've never done it."

"And how long is this supposed to last? When am I supposed to go back to my house and get pants?!"

"I'm sure it's just like a day or two."

"Really? Because he doesn't say in his little note."

Jackson furrowed his brow and grabbed the note. While he re-read the letter, I joined the crowd at the back of the bus.

Jackson looked up. "Wait, what are you doing?"

"I'm getting Perfect Potty Island back!" I yelled as I jumped.

CHAPTER FIVE

MAYOR PARFAIT

Mayor Parfait lived on the nice side of the island with all the snobby, rich people. Jackson and I glided straight to his house and knocked on the front door. No answer. I knocked louder. "Mayor! Excuse me, Mayor!"

Footsteps. Then silence.

"We'd like to have a word with you, please!" I tried.

"The mayor will be available at City Hall during normal business hours!" the mayor called out in his squeaky voice. "Please return at a later time."

"People blew up my house," I replied.

"I apologize for the inconvenience."

"Can we stay with you?" Jackson asked.

"Again, City Hall will be open during normal business hours. You are encouraged to bring your concern at that time."

I looked at Jackson. "Now what?"

Jackson looked both ways, smiled, then reached into his backpack and pulled out a pickax that looked much too big to come out of such a small bag.

I gasped. "Where did you get that?!"

"You have one too," Jackson said as he started hacking at the mayor's front door.

Crack. Crack. Crack.

"Stop!" the mayor cried. Jackson didn't stop.

Crack. Crack. Crack.

"Wait!" I yelled. Jackson didn't wait.

Crack. Crack. CRACK!

We were in. "Hi!" Jackson waved as he passed the mayor.

"I'm so sorry," I apologized.

The mayor tried to step in front of Jackson. "You can't be in here!"

Jackson squeezed past the mayor, walked up the stairs, opened the mayor's bedroom door, and turned to me. "Pick out a pair of pants."

"I don't think I can do that."

The mayor hustled up the stairs, red-faced and panting. "You can't destroy my house and take my pants without asking!"

"Why not?" Jackson asked. "You let people destroy our houses and take our island without asking."

I was about to apologize again, but I stopped. Jackson kind of had a point. We all stared at each other. Finally, I spoke up. "Uh, can I borrow a pair of pants?"

The mayor glanced at my boxers, then sighed. "Just not the gray ones. Those are my favorites."

"Take the gray ones," Jackson said.

"No!" Mayor Parfait yelled.

"They destroyed his house!"

"It rebuilds itself after every battle!" the mayor countered.

Jackson cocked his pickax behind his head like he was going to destroy the mayor's dresser.

"Wait! OK, fine. He can have the gray pants."

I smiled and put on the pants.

"Now, can you please leave?"

"Not until you tell us what's going on," I said.

"I think the letter was pretty clear."

"No, but seriously! What is this?"

"OK, before I start, I would like to remind you that this is an excellent opportunity for our community. Did you know that we will have enough funds to install a golf course soon?"

"Will we be able to golf without someone trying to kill us?"

"No one's trying to kill anyone."

Just then we heard the *rat-tat-tat* of a machine gun outside.

"Actually, why don't we step away from the window?" the mayor suggested.

"People have been trying to kill us all day!"

"Have you tried asking them to stop?"

"MULTIPLE TIMES!"

"Hm, that's odd. Vincenzo said that wouldn't happen."

"Who's Vincenzo?"

Mayor Parfait lit up. "Oh, Vincenzo del Hugo is a delightful fellow! You boys haven't met him yet?"

We stood with our arms crossed.

The mayor continued. "He's new to the island. You may have noticed the beautiful home he recently built into the side of that mountain over there."

"Wait," Jackson said. "Are you talking about the evil scientist guy?"

"He is a scientist, but I don't know why you would call him an 'evil scientist.' That seems mean."

"His house looks like a skull."

"No, it doesn't!"

Jackson pointed out the window. Mayor Parfait peeked out and then looked back at us. "Well, I'll be."

Rat-tat-tat-tat-tat!

The mayor quickly backed away from the window. "I still don't think that's fair to call him an 'evil' scientist. I don't even know what that means."

"It's a scientist who does evil things."

"Well, then, no. I am happy to report that he is not an evil scientist."

"He invited people here to destroy our island."

"No one is destroying anything."

Just then, we heard a *crack crack crack* on the roof.

"Is someone breaking in?" Jackson asked.

The mayor shrugged. "Instead of focusing on that, I think you boys need to focus on the future."

Crack. Crack. CRACK!

At that moment, a special forces ranger dropped out of the ceiling across the room. Before he hit the floor, however, a bed of spikes sprung from the ground and killed him. Jackson and I looked at the mayor with huge eyes as the ranger got zapped up in white light.

"See?" Mayor Parfait said. "By focusing on the future, I made the wise choice to install a spike trap in my home. I strongly encourage all citizens of Perfect Potty..." the mayor caught himself, held up a finger, and smiled "...*Battle* Island to invest in one for their own home."

"And you don't see a problem with any of this?" I asked.

Mayor Parfait shook his head. "I trust Vincenzo, and frankly, I am disappointed that you two do not."

"Even if you trust him, there's no way you can trust all these psychos running around, right?"

"Wow, more hurtful names coming out of your mouth."

"They're dressed up like crazy people!"

"Vincenzo allows battle royale contestants to purchase custom costumes, parachutes, and gliders with Vincenzo Bucks, or 'V-Bucks' as he calls them!

They're adorable little gold coins. I think I have one to show you." They mayor started digging through his pocket. I stopped him.

"We really don't care what the V-bucks look like. We just want to make sure this is all going to end sometime."

"Of course, it's going to end!" Mayor Parfait looked offended that I would even suggest otherwise.

"When?"

"Vincenzo said it'd be over in good time."

"What does that mean?"

"When the time is good." Mayor Parfait gave me a look that silently scolded me for asking such a dumb question.

I was about to ask more questions, but the room suddenly got dark, and I felt little pricks on my skin like someone was poking me over and over with a fistful of toothpicks. I rubbed my arm and glanced outside. The sky was dark and purple. I jabbed my thumb toward the window. "Wanna tell us what this is all about?"

"Oh! That's the storm. It's new too. I should have probably put that in the letter."

"A purple storm? How does that work?"

"I'm not sure. You'll have to ask Vincenzo. But you two should probably be leaving now."

"And why's that?"

"Well, technically, the storm will kill you if you stay in it for too long, but the good news is, you'll know where it's going with this little guy." The mayor tapped a watch on my wrist I hadn't noticed yet. "It'll give you plenty of warning so you can run away from the storm."

"No trouble at all," Jackson said dryly.

The mayor smiled. "There! That's what I'm talking about! The future is bright. Just head east, and you may be able to outrun this one."

My head started getting foggy. "Which way is east?"

Mayor Parfait said something, but I couldn't figure out what it was. I tried concentrating on his lips, but they slowly faded. The last thing I saw was a white light.

CHAPTER SIX

THE LAIR

"HE MAKES ME SO MAD!" I screamed after beaming back into the battle bus.

A gingerbread man in the seat in front of me looked back, annoyed. Jackson tried to smooth things over by pointing at me and giving a look that said, "This guy is such a spaz." The gingerbread man huffed and faced forward again. "Stop yelling. You're upsetting everyone else," Jackson whispered.

"It's going to upset me even more when they try to kill me in a few minutes! Why are you so calm about all this?!"

Jackson shrugged. "Nothing cool ever happens around here, you know? This is just a super weird break from work."

That answer annoyed me so much that I let out a yell. "Ahhhh!" My outburst earned me another disapproving look from Gingerbread.

"Maybe just chill a little bit and enjoy the ride," Jackson said. "You even have pants now! What do you have to worry about?"

"I just… I can't… But…" I stuttered, angry at myself for my inability to come up with a response for why I wouldn't want people shooting at me all day.

"See? Relaaaaaaaaax."

"I might be able to relax a little if I knew when this was going to end."

"Then why don't we ask him ourselves?"

"Ask who? Vincenzo?!"

Jackson got up. "Sure, we'll head to his place."

My palms got sweaty. "Wait! Like, shouldn't we make an appointment or something?"

"We literally just axed our way into the mayor's house. I don't think we need appointments anymore." With that, Jackson jumped.

Despite my better judgment, I followed him. We glided to the mountain, then circled the hideout. Jackson headed straight for one of the windows.

“Shouldn’t we knock on the front door?” I asked.

Jackson ignored me and dipped into the open window. I peeked over my shoulder to make sure nobody was following us and tumbled in too. By the time I got my bearings, Jackson had already started exploring the hideout. “Look at all this cool stuff!”

“We shouldn’t be here!” I hissed.

“Come on, he’s the one who gave everyone gliders and pickaxes. He has to be cool with people breaking into his house. Right, Mr. Del Hugo?” Jackson waited for an answer. No reply. “Ha!” he turned to me. “I knew he wouldn’t be here.”

“Why?”

“If you knew this was going to happen, would you stick around?”

“Then why did we come?”

“I always wanted to check this place out.”

I glared at Jackson.

“It’s not so bad,” Jackson said. “Like this part. What’s so scary about this?”

I took a break from glaring to check out the room. I had to admit, it wasn't too bad. Just a bunch of classic cars. Maybe Vincenzo was just a dad who liked to work on old cars in his free time. Maybe we misjudged him. Maybe...

Oh boy.

We rounded the corner, and any thought I'd had about Vincenzo being a good guy went right out the window. Because right there in the middle of the lair was an enormous missile.

"Maybe it's a spaceship?" Jackson tried.

I leaned in to get a closer look at the words on the side. Danger. Explosive. Radioactive.

HISSSSSSSS!

I jumped back as steam puffed out the bottom.

"Let's go," I said. "Now."

Jackson grinned, but I could tell the grin was a little more strained. He was starting to get scared too, but he didn't want it to show. "Hey now, this is just getting good." Jackson crept to the control panel.

I looked over his shoulder. There were enough buttons, lights, and screens to, well, launch a rocket. There was also a creepy old clock right in the middle of everything for some reason. "I'm leaving."

"OK."

"Seriously!"

"Suit yourself. I'm going to check out the upper levels."

"No!"

Jackson ignored me and started walking up the stairs. I looked back at the exit, then ran toward Jackson.

He turned and smiled. "I thought you were leaving."

"I'm not going to let you get killed in here by yourself."

"How sweet."

When we turned the corner to the second level, I bumped into a gurney and almost jumped out of my skin. Jackson laughed. "You scared of a bed now?"

"It has straps to hold people down!"

"Yeah, it's from a hospital."

"Or a torture chamber."

We kept walking. On the third level, we found a stash of weapons. I grabbed a pistol, although I knew it wouldn't do me any good since I was shaking so much. Jackson grabbed some grenades.

The fourth level didn't have much of anything besides a supply closet and a terrifying view of the missile. We took a minute to appreciate how big it was. "What do you think he plans on doing with it?" I asked.

Jackson shrugged. "Maybe it's a big firework." Then Jackson turned around and leaned over the other side of the platform. "Oh cool!"

I followed his pointing. Way down below was a pool. It wasn't your average underground lair swimming pool, though. This one had black water and a tangle of wires snaking into it.

"How cool would it be to have a pool inside your house?" Jackson asked.

"The water's black."

"Nothing a little chlorine can't fix."

I was about to argue, but then I noticed a ripple in the water. I grabbed the railing tighter. "Shhh!"

"What?"

"Did you see that?"

"In the pool? You can't see anything from way up here!"

"SHHH!"

I could tell Jackson had a retort on the tip of his tongue, but he stopped himself. He saw it too. We stared at the black water, and then something happened that almost sent us both over the edge of the railing.

RIIIIIIING!

A shrill ringtone pierced the silence.

"Turn off your phone!" I yelled.

RIIIIIIING!

"I said, 'Turn it off!'"

"It's not mine!"

RIIIIIIING!

"Well, it's not mine! These aren't even my pants!"

RIIIIIIING!

I stopped and noticed the vibrating in my pocket. My heart sank. Mayor Parfait's phone. I pulled it out, looked at the screen, and saw the last name I wanted to see.

Vincenzo.

CHAPTER SEVEN

FORTNIGHT

"Hello?"

I stared at Jackson in horror. Before I could toss the phone into the pool, Jackson had snatched it out of my hands and answered like it was no big deal.

"I said 'hello'!" Jackson repeated. He switched to speakerphone mode and held out the phone. I thought I heard breathing coming from the other end. Finally, someone spoke.

"This not mayor?" an old, crackly voice asked.

"It's the mayor's assistant," Jackson lied. "Who's this?"

No answer.

"Hello?"

Finally, a low chuckle came from the other end. "Enjoying game?"

"Hang up!" I mouthed. "Hang. Up."

"It's OK," Jackson said. "We were just wondering when everything would go back to normal."

More breathing. "So… not enjoying game?"

"We'd be able to enjoy it more if we knew when it would end."

Before Jackson finished his sentence, the voice started coughing. The cough went on for an uncomfortably long time, then it morphed into a hack like Vincenzo was trying to muster up a loogie in his throat. Finally, he settled down and uttered a single word.

"Fortnight."

"Excuse me?" Jackson asked.

"One fortnight to win. If not, island…" Vincenzo stopped to hack out a lung for another five minutes. "Island mine."

Before Jackson could ask his next question, he got interrupted by a sound.

HISSSSSSSSS!

It was the missile again! Jackson jumped, almost dropped the phone over the edge, then hung it up. We both breathed heavily for a few moments before Jackson broke the silence.

"Well, there you go," he said. "You have a whole fortnight to win a game! 'Fortnight' is like Shakespeare speak for two weeks, right? That's nothing!"

"HE'S GONNA KILL US!" I yelled.

"Don't be dramatic."

"HE KNOWS WE'RE HERE, AND HE'S GONNA KILL US!"

"I'm sure he just…"

RIIIIIIIING!

Jackson instinctively threw the phone down when it started ringing in his hands.

I looked at the caller ID. Vincenzo. "SEE?!"

RIIIIIIIING!

I stuck out my foot to scoot the phone over the

ledge, but before I could, the phone did something I'd never seen in my life.

It answered itself.

"Where?" the voice asked.

We remained silent, waiting for the whole question. The voice finally repeated itself more firmly. "Where."

"Uh, hi," Jackson said. "Sorry about that. Looks like we got disconnected. Reception here is not…"

"WHERE?!" the voice growled. I cringed.

"City hall!" Jackson lied. "We're at city hall! Someone, uh, just flushed a toilet."

More silence. Then low cackling. "Lie."

"No, it's the truth!" Jackson insisted.

"Lie."

"I'm telling you…"

"Final chance," Vincenzo interrupted.

Now, it was Jackson's turn to breathe into the phone.

"If lie, you meet Raven. Raven bring death. Forever death."

Jackson looked at me. I put my hands up. We were in too deep now. This was all on Jackson.

"I'm sorry if you think I'm lying, but I'm not."

Silence.

"OK?"

More silence.

"Um, I'm going to hang up now."

"No," Vincenzo said. "Waiting."

"Waiting for what?"

Suddenly, Jackson got his answer. The old clock downstairs struck noon, and a giant, disheveled cuckoo bird popped out.

"CUCKOO! CUCKOO!" it screamed, erasing all doubt as to where we might be.

Vincenzo did that low chuckle again. "I was hoping."

"CUCKOO! CUCKOO!"

Jackson kicked the phone off the ledge. "Run!" We started sprinting down the stairs.

"CUCKOO! CUCKOO!"

Suddenly, the whole place flashed purple. "What was that?!"

"CUCKOO! CUCKOO!"

I sneaked a peek over the ledge and slammed on the brakes. Jackson bumped into me. "MOVE!" he yelled.

"No, look!"

"CUCKOO! CUCKOO!"

We both leaned over the railing to see that the water in the pool below was now glowing purple.

"CUCKOO! CUCKOO!"

The cuckoo finally finished its twelfth screech, but instead of going back into the clock, it hopped off its perch and strolled across the room into the pool. Jackson and I didn't dare move. As soon as the bird jumped into the pool, huge bolts of electricity arced over the water. That went on for a few seconds, then — *BOOM!* The power went out. The only light in the whole place came from the glowing purple water. Slowly, a human-shaped figure started to emerge from the water. The figure was black from head-to-toe except for a pair of white wings on its back. It had black armor with black raven feathers on its shoulders. Oh, and its eyes glowed green.

I didn't realize I'd been holding my breath until the creature locked eyes with me. That's when I screamed.

The Raven started building a tower up to us. All the building I'd seen before was fast, but this was insane lightning speed.

KACHUNK! KACHUNK! KACHUNK!

It took him two seconds to get up to the third level. One more second, and he'd reach us. I readied my pistol with one shaky hand, but Jackson had different ideas. He grabbed my arm and jumped off the ledge. As I fell, I felt wildly for my glider but came up empty. Then…

BAM!

I hit the ground so hard I blacked out.

CHAPTER EIGHT

TAR

Back in the bus, Jackson's face was completely white. "I'm sorry, I'm sorry! I had no idea that would happen!"

I just shook my head. I was so furious that I didn't even want to talk to Jackson.

"But, hey, all we have to do to get the island back is win one game!" Jackson said, trying to smooth things over "That's good news, right?"

I sat stonefaced.

Jackson poked my side. "Right?"

"Oh yeah, great news!" I finally said. "Learning that I'm being hunted by the angel of death was the highlight of my day! Can't think of anything better!"

"It's not ideal..."

"Forever death. Did you hear that? FOREVER death!"

"I heard, OK? I heard. But if we win a game, he goes away, right?"

I threw up my hands. "Who knows?! Hey, I have an idea, why don't we call Crazy Brains again to ask if he'll clarify!"

"I said I'm sorry!"

I folded my arms. "Sometimes, sorry doesn't cut it." I sulked while two girls in pink bear suits whispered and pointed across the aisle at me. Jackson finally stood up and walked to the back of the bus.

"Where do you think you're going?" I asked.

Jackson shrugged. "One of us has got to get out there." With that, he dove. I sulked awhile longer, then got up and jumped too.

I lost Jackson in all the colorful characters dotting the sky, but I didn't care. I aimed for my house. I was going to put on my own pants, sit in my own bedroom, and come up with my own plan for getting out of this mess.

By the time I landed, Pinecrest Park was already swarming with activity. One of the pink bears was running through my back door. A soccer player was locked in a vicious shotgun fight with a basketball player. *BOOM!* Someone just blew up half of Jackson's house. That made me smile a little. After a moment, I finally decided to check out a treasure chest stashed under one of the trees on the outskirts of town, then I was going to hide until it was safe to go back into my house.

My heart beat fast as I ran. I wouldn't dare tell Jackson this, but I actually felt a little invigorated. As long as I avoided the Raven, the guns weren't real. And if the guns weren't real, this was basically laser tag, right? I'd only played laser tag once as a kid, but I remember being pretty good at it. Granted, I was playing against other seven-year-olds at a birthday party, but still.

I reached the chest without anyone seeing me and opened it up. An assault rifle, grenade, and small vial of blue liquid popped out. I had no idea what the blue liquid was, but it was clearly meant for drinking, so I dabbed a drop on my tongue to make sure it tasted OK. Ooh! Blue raspberry! I chugged it and felt a cool tingle wash over my body. I tried to touch my arm, but couldn't seem to make contact with my skin thanks to some sort of invisible force field. So the blue stuff was like a shield? Cool!

I collected the weapons and crept around the tree to get a better view of my house. That plan didn't last long.

"Pete!" Mailman Dale called out.

I quickly retreated back behind the tree. "Oh, uh, now is not..."

"I see you found some pants!" Dale chuckled as he practically bounced toward me. "Hey, are you ever going to grab your mail?"

"Yes, Dale. Now, I really need..."

"Oh good. You know I hate to be a pest, but..."

POP!

I peeked out just in time to see poor Dale get beamed up by the light, courtesy of an army guy with a silenced pistol. The army guy didn't see me, so I slowly brought my gun to my shoulder, reminding myself the whole time this wasn't real. I aimed, then squeezed the trigger.

BANG! BANG! BANG!

All of my shots missed wildly, but they did alert the army guy to my exact position.

POP!

I felt my shield melt away.

POP! POP! POP!

The army guy continued to shoot as I ran as fast as I could toward my house, zigging and zagging and jumping the whole way, hoping that the army guy was just as bad of a shot as I was. After what felt like an eternity, I finally reached my house, pulled the mail out of the box to make Dale happy, threw open the door, and…

…Almost threw up.

The place was covered in putrid black tar. I looked up and froze when I saw the source of the tar.

It was the Raven.

CHAPTER NINE

THE BUSH

As soon as I stepped into the house, the Raven raised his black gun and squeezed the trigger.

BAM!

The Raven's bullet slammed into a brick wall that had magically appeared in front of my face. Before I even realized what was going on, a hand grabbed my arm and pulled me outside. It was Jackson. He opened his mouth to tell me something, but...

POP! POP! POP!

The army guy got him first. I backed against the house and put my hands up, waiting for the army guy to pop me too, but he never got a chance.

BAM!

The Raven broke through the brick wall and blasted the army guy. I recoiled in shock when I saw what happened to him — he instantly turned black and started melting. There was no white light in sight.

The Raven had shot from inside the house, meaning he hadn't seen me yet. I had one, maybe two seconds before he walked out that door. I hugged the house and backpedaled away from the door while pulling a grenade out of my bag. *You can do this,* I reminded myself.

But then the Raven emerged, and I absolutely did not do it. Instead, I got scared, tripped, and let go of the grenade. It blew up in my face.

Back on the bus, Jackson grabbed me. "I can't believe you made it!"

"What..." I tried to catch my breath. "What happened?"

"I noticed you running for your house, so I started shooting that guy who was chasing you. I backed up against your house, and I heard something move inside. Just before you got to the door, I peeked inside and saw that Raven thing. I didn't have time to warn you, so I threw up a wall real quick."

I shook my head. "Thanks, man."

Jackson looked concerned. "Hey, if we're going to pull this off, we need to stick together. Deal?"

I looked him in the eye and nodded. "Deal."

"Then let's get to work."

Jackson and I spent the next several hours figuring out the game. We learned to rely on our watches to show us where the storm was heading and how many players remained. We learned to rely on our ears to keep us away from gunfights. We learned to rely on each other for moral support. Most of all, though, we learned that we could absolutely not rely on our shooting skills.

Here's a scene that played out multiple times throughout those first few hours:

"There! Right down there!" I'd whisper excitedly in Jackson's ear.

"I see him!" Jackson would then pull out a sniper rifle and aim.

I'd rub my hands together. Our first kill! How exciting! Jackson would take a deep breath and slowly let it out like he'd learned in some war movie, then…

BANG!

...Miss the guy completely.

I'd always fool myself into thinking it was OK since we were so far away from the enemy. But without fail, the guy would build his way over to our hideout, then totally destroy both of us in less time than it took for Jackson to load another bullet into his sniper rifle.

Slowly, a new strategy started to form. Hide-and-seek.

Jackson and I started living by three rules — outrun the storm, avoid anything that even looked like the Raven, and don't come within 100 feet of anyone holding a gun. We would sneak from basements to bushes to bathrooms, making stealth our number one priority. A few games into this new strategy, we found a prize that seemed to be the missing piece of the puzzle. Jackson opened a treasure chest outside an abandoned house, and a glowing bush sprang out.

"What's that?" I asked.

Jackson shrugged and grabbed the bush. Suddenly, he disappeared inside of it.

I freaked out. "YOU JUST TURNED INTO A BUSH!"

"What?" he asked, his voice muffled by the leaves.

"You're a bush with legs! This is like the greatest prize in the whole game!" I was giddy with excitement. "Wait, wait, wait, try to crouch."

Jackson crouched. His legs disappeared, and all I saw was an ordinary bush. I shook my head. "I don't see how we can lose now."

We did lose. Almost immediately. While Jackson looked exactly like a bush when he crouched, he looked exactly like the biggest dweeb you've ever seen when he ran away from the storm. People figured out what was going on pretty quickly when they saw a guy escorting a bush all over the island.

"OK, duck here," I told Jackson when we reached a ridge. "I'm going to hide behind you, and..."

Chink chink chink

A grenade bounced in front of us.

"YIPES!"

BANG!

Back to the battle bus.

The failed bush experiment only added fuel to our hide-and-seek strategy. "I've got a spot!" Jackson said. "You know the house that Mr. Emerson built in the middle of the lake?"

"Oh yeah!" I high-fived Jackson. "Nobody would ever think to go there!"

Turns out, about six people think to go there every game. The one time we had the house to ourselves, the storm immediately closed in, and we got shot trying to hop our way across the shallow lake.

"What if we hide under the water?" I suggested.

Jackson's eyes lit up. "And build little homemade snorkels?"

"Foolproof!"

As you may have guessed, the plan was far from foolproof. All it did was get us super wet and provide endless entertainment for the people shooting at us. "Unnnng," I said after the fourth time we died in the water. "I heard them laughing all the way across the lake that time."

Our final stroke of genius was landing inside a tree. The first and only time we tested that idea, someone came by, chopped down the tree, and dropped us to our death.

It took us a while, but we eventually perfected our strategy. By hugging the edge of the storm, we could consistently stay hidden until the top 10 people. But guess what? Nobody gets a prize for being in the top 10. And without fail, every time we made it that far, someone in a giant tower would spot us and take us out.

"They see everything!" Jackson complained back in the bus after yet another tower goon killed us.

I just smushed my face against the window, too exhausted to respond. I stared at the tiny towns and farms below, wondering if we'd ever luck into the right hiding spot. Suddenly, my eyes snapped open. Of course! I turned to Jackson and smiled.

"They don't see *everything*."

CHAPTER TEN

SKYBASE

"My arms feel like noodles!" Jackson complained. "Do we really need to keep chopping?"

"More chopping, less whining!"

Early in our quest, we'd learned that chopping stuff with our pickaxes didn't just let us break through walls; it also gave us material we could use to build on our own. And no matter how much building material we carried, our backpacks didn't feel any heavier. We'd mostly ignored building before because we hadn't understood how it worked and it didn't help us hide any better, but that was all about to change.

"All the trees are gone over here," Jackson said.

"Then start on the bushes!"

Once we really started chopping, I was delighted

to learn that our pickaxes were strong enough to take out anything — houses, cars, semi-trucks, even rocks.

"The storm's closing in," Jackson said. "You wanna finally tell me what you plan to do with all this stuff?"

"Two words: Sky. Base."

"Excuse me?"

"A sky base! People keep finding us because they're higher than us, right?"

"I guess."

I grinned. "Not anymore. We now have enough material to build a ramp up to the clouds. Maybe above the clouds! We just build a ramp as tall as we can, wait for everybody else to kill each other, then pick off the last guy before he spots us."

Jackson stared at me. "Pete."

"Yeah?"

"You come up with a lot of bad ideas."

"I wouldn't say 'a lot.'"

"But then sometimes, you really outdo yourself."

A smile spread across his face. "This is genius. Pure GENIUS!"

"See! I knew you would be on board!"

"Oh man, I can't believe no one has had this idea sooner!"

We waited until most of the other contestants had eliminated each other, then started constructing our sky base. We cackled to each other as we built higher and higher until all the people below were tiny specks.

I finally stopped for breath. "How much material do you have left?"

"Plenty!" Jackson yelled.

"Shhhh! People are right below us."

"They can't hear us," Jackson said. "See? HooooWHEEEEEE!"

I cringed, but nobody looked up. "HAHAHAHA!" I doubled over with glee. "HoooooоWHEEEEEEE!"

We looked down. Seven people remained in the game — us and five others. Then four others. The storm closed in a little closer. Three left. Then two. Finally, there was just one other player left. An old-timey detective. From the safety of our epic skybase, we watched him look around, confused about where two more people could be hiding.

"You should do the honors," Jackson said.

I reached into my backpack, but unfortunately, I had forgotten to collect any weapons. "Looks like it's all you."

Jackson drew a small pistol. "Hey, buddy!" he screamed. "Feast on this!"

Bang! Bang! Bang!

He missed badly. Jackson winked at me. "Don't worry, I have plenty of ammo left."

Bang! Bang! Bang!

Not even close. Jackson's victim finally looked up when he heard the gunshots. "Watch out!" I warned.

"Relax," Jackson said. "We definitely have the advantage here."

Bang! Bang! Bang!

I squinted at the detective below. He wasn't even shooting. In fact, he seemed to be… dancing? "I have a bad feeling about this," I said.

The detective finally took out a sniper rifle, but instead of pointing it at us, he aimed far away, back where we'd started building our ramp.

CRACK!

Jackson laughed. "Almost, buddy! Here, I'll give you a target!" He then wiggled his butt in the direction of our enemy. I was about to tell Jackson to cool it when I heard an ominous sound.

Chunkchunkchunkchunk

"What's that?" Jackson asked.

ChunkchunkchunkCHUNKCHUNKCHUNK!

Suddenly, I saw it. The single sniper shot had taken out the bottom of our skybase, and now the entire structure was crumbling from the ground up.

"GET DOWN! GO, GO, GO!"

"I ONLY KNOW HOW TO BUILD UP!"

We frantically dug through our backpacks until the chunking caught up to us and the last piece of our glorious skybase disintegrated under our feet. I tried to deploy my glider as I fell, but it wouldn't come out of my backpack. I sadly watched the detective run underneath our fall so he could dance on our dead bodies when we landed.

"Why couldn't we glide down?" I asked Jackson back on the bus.

"You're not allowed to pull out your glider unless you jump off a launchpad or something," Jackson said.

I rolled my eyes. "What a dumb rule."

The next game, we actually found a launchpad to place on our skybase, but we got shot out of the sky before we were able to use it. We tried three more skybases after that, and each ended more disastrously than the last. "You know," I said as we prepared for construction on our sixth skybase. "Maybe there's a reason more people don't try this."

Jackson wasn't paying attention to me.

"Hello," I said, waving in front of his face.

He just pointed. "New idea."

I followed his finger. He was pointing to a shopping cart.

CHAPTER ELEVEN

DALE

"This is so stupid," I repeated for the hundredth time as I pushed the shopping cart up the mountain.

Jackson cackled from inside the cart. "You know you love it."

We were both right. I did love the idea, but our stunt was very, very stupid. Our goal was to use a shopping cart to launch ourselves down a mountain, off a ramp, over a canyon, and into a fort we'd built on the other side.

Now, you might be wondering what this possibly has to do with winning the battle royale. Um, well, it had certainly started out as a way to win the contest. Jackson's original idea was to use the shopping cart to carry more weapons up to our skybase. Although we quickly learned that we weren't able to store weapons in the shopping cart, we also learned that pushing a shopping cart down a skybase ramp is great fun. And do you know what's even more fun than that? Sitting inside a shopping cart while it's rocketing down a skybase ramp. Once we rode down the skybase a few times, our natural next step was building a launch ramp at the bottom of the run. And when the launch ramp worked, well, what else could we do but try bigger and bigger ramps until we constructed something capable of launching us over the canyon. Finally, Jackson made the life-changing discovery that we could get a nice speed boost by firing a rocket launcher from inside the shopping cart.

But to answer your original question, no. This stunt had absolutely nothing to do with winning a battle royale.

"Why don't you duck this time, so you don't take another rocket to the face?" Jackson asked when we reached the top of the mountain.

"Obviously." Then, I kicked the ground a few times and held on for dear life.

We rumbled down the mountain faster and faster, then hit the jump perfectly. When we finally got airborne, I ducked, Jackson launched his rocket, and we really blasted off. I sneaked a peek at the canyon below when our flight reached its highest point, and I got a little lightheaded. This was so, so stupid.

"We're gonna make it!" Jackson screamed.

As we neared the end of our jump, I braced for impact. Then, *WHAM!* We slammed into the fort floor, bounced a few times, then skidded safely to a stop.

"Woohoo!" we both yelled as we jumped out of the cart. Jackson pumped his fist in the air over and over like he'd just won the Super Bowl. When we finally stopped to catch our breath, we heard a strange sound. Clapping.

"Nicely done!"

We spun around, suddenly aware that we were unarmed. I put up my fists.

"Goodness gracious, you boys are something else!"

I lowered my fists. "Oh. Hi, Dale."

Mailman Dale, just as chipper as ever, shoved a fistful of letters into my hand. "You know, if you don't plan on checking your mail that often, the post office offers reasonable rates on P.O. boxes."

I looked at the letters, confused. "Are these all from one day? I emptied the mailbox right after we talked yesterday."

Dale shook his head. "It's been a week at least. Maybe a week and a half."

I got a sharp panic twinge in my stomach. No way. We hadn't been at this that long at all. But as I flipped through the mail, that panic turned to sinking dread. Somehow, the dates were a week and a half later than I'd expected. I looked up at Dale with a million questions in my eyes. He shrugged.

"Time seems to be moving a lot faster since the costumed folks landed on the island."

"What's going on?" Jackson asked me.

BAM!

Before I could answer, a bullet struck our fort. I looked over and gasped. The wall that had been hit was turning black.

"It's him!" I hissed at Jackson.

Jackson's eyes got wide.

BAM! BAM!

The wall started melting before my eyes.

"The cart!" Jackson yelled.

I nodded, threw up another wall for protection, then turned to Dale. "You have to get in there with Jackson!"

"Oh no, I'm no daredevil."

BAM!

"Trust me!" I shoved Dale into the cart.

BAM!

With Jackson and Dale inside, I grabbed the cart and started running. Just outside our fort was a cliff. If I ran fast enough, maybe I could push us all over the cliff before getting killed by the Raven.

But as soon as I emerged from the fort, Dale panicked. "What are you doing?!" he screamed. And before I could stop him, he dove out of the cart.

"DALE!" I tried to grab him, but the shopping cart's momentum carried Jackson and me off the cliff before I could reach him.

BAM!

The last thing I saw before I hit the ground was my mailman turning black as tar.

Back on the bus, I put my head in my hands, and Jackson stared at the floor glumly. Dale was dead — probably forever dead — and we had no one to blame but ourselves. On top of that, only three days remained to win a battle royale, and we'd yet to even get a single kill. I wanted to throw up. "This is impossible," I finally said.

"It's not," Jackson tried. "We can… How about…" He fell silent when he realized he didn't have any answers.

"We're just getting destroyed out there. We need more time to get better."

"Or we need to get better faster," Jackson suggested.

"Yeah, and how does that happen? Magic? We spend 20 minutes every game finding weapons, then get slaughtered as soon as we run into someone."

"We drop into the action right away."

"Oh, really?" I jabbed my finger at the window. "That's a big island. People spread out."

"Let's just sit back and see."

So we did. We deployed our gliders the second we left the bus, and a guy dressed in a dinosaur suit immediately flew past us screaming, "TIIIIIIII!"

I looked at Jackson. "What did he say?"

Then a lady in camo gear screamed past. "TILLLLLLLLLLL!"

"What are you saying?!" I yelled after her.

Then a pack of twenty people all followed, yelling the same thing in unison.

"TILLLLLLLLLLLLLLLLLLLLLTEEEEEEEEE EEEEEED!"

CHAPTER TWELVE

TILTED TOWERS

"Tilted Towers." That's what they were calling it. I had no idea why. Sure, the city has towers. Newberry Heights is the largest city on our little island, and it's filled with office towers and apartment buildings. But not one of them is remotely tilted. I tried asking about it once.

"Excuse me," I asked a scuba diver wielding a pickax. "Do you know why people call this place, 'Tilted Towers?'"

The diver turned and started whacking me with his pickax.

Whack! Whack! Whack!

"Wait!" I tried running away. "It's just that everything looks straight!"

Whack! Whack! Whack!

"You're not curious?!"

Whack! Whack! WHACK!

I curled into a ball just in time to get sucked up by the white light. I don't think there's anything in life more humiliating than death by pickax.

"Why do you think everyone comes here?" Jackson asked the next time we landed in the city.

"No idea. It's not like..."

BANG!

I got shot by someone on another building.

We tried it again.

"It's not like there aren't other places on the island. A whole bunch of..."

BANG!

We died again.

"A whole bunch of other areas have just as much loot without nearly as many angry..."

BANG!

We died over and over and over. As the first of our three days turned into night, I started worrying that maybe we were wasting our time. Were we doomed to an eternity of getting blasted by jerks in apartment buildings?

But slowly, ever so slowly, things started turning around. My first kill came when I found a shotgun sitting next to some kid's bed. I grabbed it, then immediately got whacked in the back with a pickax.

Whack! Whack! Whack!

I turned and screamed. It was a full-grown man in an ill-fitting Easter bunny suit. "Stop!" I yelled.

Whack! Whack! Whack!

I backed up until I hit the wall, then fell to the ground.

Whack! Whack! Whack!

I closed my eyes, knowing that one more whack would finish me off. Then I pulled the trigger.

BANG!

The Easter bunny disappeared in a flash of light.

"Woohoo!"

I celebrated with a dance. Then a guy with a hamburger for a head dropped through the roof and killed me with a single whack.

While I struggled to luck into a single kill, Jackson was quickly turning into a Navy SEAL. He learned how to use a shotgun, machine gun, and well-placed spike trap to clear an entire apartment building. We eventually settled into a nice groove where Jackson would do all the hard work, and I'd offer encouragement.

"Nice shot!" I called out one time from inside a bathtub.

"LITTLE HELP PLEASE!" Jackson yelled as he reloaded.

I poked my head out of the tub. "You're doing gr…"

BANG! BANG! Dead.

Back in the bus, Jackson shook his head at me. "You've got to pull your weight!"

"I'm watching your back!"

"You're hiding."

"I prefer to think of it as stealth. Also, I'm super encouraging." I wiggled my eyebrows to get Jackson to smile. He didn't.

"I need you out there, OK?" Jackson finally said. "I can't do this by myself."

I sighed and nodded. We dropped in again, and I got serious. Notice I said "serious" not "good." I still died a lot, but now I was at least trying to be a productive member of the team by rolling around corners and sneaking in a shot or two before getting killed. Slowly, though, ever so slowly, I started getting better. I discovered that a machine gun could help make up for my poor aim. I learned to listen for people running up stairs so I could surprise them at just the right moment. I got good at covering Jackson's back while he covered mine. By working together, we started clearing two or three apartment buildings each game. One time, we tore through five different towers before Jackson stopped and held his finger to his mouth.

I paused and listened. Nothing. I gave Jackson a quizzical look.

"It's empty," Jackson said.

"What's empty?"

"The city."

I gasped, then did a dance and howled at the sky. "I AM THE KING OF TILTED TOWERS!"

CRACK!

Someone immediately sniped me from the hills outside the city.

Jackson quickly died too and appeared next to me back on the bus. "I'm feeling good about this next game," he said. "Really good."

"Where are we dropping?" I asked.

"Clock tower."

We strode to the back of the bus together like we owned the place, then rocketed toward the ground, screaming in unison. "TILLLLLLTED!"

I opened my glider a few seconds before Jackson did so I could scout out our opponents' landing spots. No one else looked like they were headed for the clock tower, which meant we'd have all the loot to ourselves. I followed Jackson to the tower's roof, then slipped into the hole he'd hacked. "Hey, if you find any silenced pistols this time, can you leave them for me?" I asked. "I think I'm going to try..."

"JUMP!" Jackson screamed as he scrambled back out. I looked inside the tower, and my eyes got wide. Someone else was already there. Someone covered in head-to-toe jet-black armor. Someone with raven feathers on his shoulders.

I joined Jackson leaping to the pavement and heard the sound of a rifle behind me.

CRACK!

The ground couldn't come soon enough.

CRACK!

Almost there. I closed my eyes.

CRACK!

I gasped. A searing pain shot up my leg. Then I hit the ground and died.

CHAPTER THIRTEEN

THE STORM

Back in the battle bus, the pain wasn't any better. "MY LEG, MY LEG!" I screamed.

Jackson grabbed my shoulder. "Shhhhhh." Then he leaned in. "What happened?"

I squirmed in my seat. "He got me. Right in my leg!"

"Where?" Jackson asked as he inspected my leg. "Up here?"

"I don't know, probably where all the blood is!"

Jackson rolled up my pant leg to get a better look.

"OUCH!" I squeezed my eyes closed. "Yes, right there! Stop touching it."

"Pete, take a breath."

"I SAID TO STOP TOUCHING IT!" I screamed. Ten heads from the front of the bus turned to see what the commotion was.

"Pete." Jackson got right in my face. "Look down."

I did. There was no blood. I gasped. "Where's the bullet wound?!"

"There is no bullet wound," Jackson said.

"I'm telling you, it hurts!"

"I believe you, Pete. I believe you. Can you put weight on your leg?"

I tried to stand. "Ahhh!"

"Take your time."

I put a little bit of pressure on it. "It burns. It burns so much. Like someone's holding a blowtorch against my leg."

"Put your arm around my shoulder, and we're going to jump."

"Did you not hear one word I just said?!"

"It's going to be all right. We'll find one of those

med kits down there, then we'll patch you up as good as new."

I grimaced as we shuffled to the back of the bus. When I looked down, I saw that the bus had nearly finished its path across the island, and we were currently flying over the woods. I tried to keep my mind off the pain by focusing on the forest. Jackson and I had gone there a lot when we were kids. Right in the middle of the woods, someone had grown a hedge maze surrounding a little hideout on stilts. Jackson and I used to pretend we were the only ones in the world who knew about the hideout, even though we always found other people's trash lying on the ground.

"I'll drop you off in the hideout, then find a med kit and be back in no time. OK?"

"OK."

Jackson searched my eyes to make sure I was OK, then bent down so I could grab his shoulders. After making sure I was on tight, Jackson jumped. He looked back as soon as we left the bus. "Hold tighter! I'm opening the glider in three, two, one."

"OOF!" My arm nearly tore out of its socket when Jackson opened the glider.

I managed to hold on as we glided to the ground, then Jackson rolled over right before we touched down so he could take the brunt of the fall for me. He then carried me through the maze and plopped me inside the hideout. "You'll be safe in here. Just hang out in the corner and don't go anywhere. I'll be back soon."

"Thanks."

"You're gonna be the king of Tilted Towers again in no time."

"Can't wait."

Jackson winked and jumped out of the hideout. I breathed. Silence. For the first time since the disco music woke me up, there was true silence. I closed my eyes to block out the pain and suddenly realized I hadn't slept in a long, long time. Even with the burning in my leg, I started to drift off.

I dreamed right away. In the dream (Yes, I'm going to tell you about my dream. Deal with it), I was back in Vincenzo's evil scientist lair. I ran up the stairs on my bad leg.

THUNK! THUNK! THUNK!

The Raven followed calmly behind. It was almost as if he didn't care how far I got because he knew I was dead either way.

THUNK! THUNK! THUNK!

I shot wildly with my little revolver as I ran harder.

THUNK! THUNK! THUNK!

Finally, I reached the platform at the top of the stairs where Jackson and I had ended up earlier. I shakily pulled out my gun and prepared to duel the Raven. His steps got closer.

Thunk. Thunk. Thunk.

I leaned over the railing to gauge how close he was and caught a glimpse of the purple, glowing pool down below. Gulp. I knew what I had to do. It was a long fall, probably too long to survive, but there was just no way I could face the Raven by myself.

Thunk. Thunk. Thunk.

I took a deep breath, held my nose, then tumbled backward off the railing.

SPLASH!

I started screaming the instant I hit the pool. The

purple liquid was acid. Fizzing, burning acid.

"Ahhhh!" I woke with a jolt and instinctively tried to wipe the acid off my skin. But even in the real world, my skin continued to burn. That's when I realized the storm had closed in. Almost immediately, I had another realization: something else from my dream had come from the real world.

Thunk. Thunk. Thunk.

The noise. Someone was climbing the stairs of my hideout. Slowly. Purposefully. I tried to scrunch myself tighter into the corner. No way Jackson would be walking that slowly, especially in the storm. The steps stopped. I held my breath. Then the doorknob turned, and the door slowly creaked open. By now, my vision was hazy from the storm, but there was no mistaking my visitor. It was the Raven.

GAAAAASP!

Back on the bus. I gasped for air a couple times, feeling like I'd just woken from another dream. The good news was that the storm had taken me before the Raven was able to. But that was little comfort once I learned the bad news. The bad news — the very worst news imaginable — was that the seat next to me remained empty. Jackson hadn't returned.

CHAPTER FOURTEEN

GRAVEYARD SHOWDOWN

He's not dead. He's not dead. He's not dead.

I kept repeating those three words to myself until I believed them. No matter how slim the odds, I had to hold out hope that the Raven hadn't killed Jackson; that my best friend was still down there. If that were somehow true, it gave me one more reason to win this thing: I'd get to reunite with Jackson.

I grimaced, limped to the back of the bus, and jumped.

Hoping to avoid the Raven at all costs, I glided as far away from the woods as possible. Unfortunately, that landed me in the graveyard that I'd always suspected to be haunted. Fortunately, I was the only person who landed in the graveyard, so I took my time limping around and collecting loot. There was a pistol, bundle of wood, and... YES! A med kit!

I grabbed the kit and ducked behind a tombstone to bandage my throbbing leg. I did the best I could, then sighed when I finished. My leg didn't feel any better. Just as I was about to stand up, I heard something.

Shuffle, shuffle.

Another player had entered the graveyard. My pulse quickened. OK, this was my chance to put together everything I'd learned in the towers. I strained to listen for the sound again.

Shuffle, shuffle.

It was coming straight toward me. I equipped my pistol and slowly peeked around the tombstone. I craned my neck a little further, then...

GASP!

I spun back behind the tombstone. It was the Raven! How could he have crossed the island so fast?! And how did he know where to find me? No time for those questions now; I only had seconds to come up with a plan. Even though I'd improved my aim significantly over the past few days, I knew that trying to shoot the Raven with my little pistol would be a death sentence. If I tried to run, he'd finish me off in a second. Even if he somehow missed once or twice, I had no chance — the graveyard was surrounded by wide-open fields that offered no cover. If other players were in the area, then I could at least try to get killed by someone else, but no one else was around for miles. It was just me.

Shuffle, shuffle.

The Raven had almost reached my gravestone when I saw it. Sitting just outside the graveyard like a gift from heaven was a grenade. If I could only reach the grenade, I could blow myself up before the Raven reached me.

Shuffle, shuffle.

I glanced at my watch to check my stats. I had enough wood for four walls. Was that enough cover to reach the grenade? I was about to find out. I threw up the first wall and started sprinting.

BANG! BANG!

The Raven took out my wall in two shots. I built the second wall behind me without breaking stride.

BANG! BANG!

That one went too. I was about to throw up my third wall, but I noticed that the shooting had stopped. I sneaked a peek behind me to see something terrifying — the Raven was building a ramp! He was done trying to shoot through my walls, he'd just shoot over them. I put my head down and ran harder. Almost there!

BANG!

I instinctively built a wall behind me.

BANG!

The second bullet hit the ground inches from my foot and sprayed dirt in my face. I fell down and accidentally built my last wall as a ceiling above me.

BANG! BANG!

The Raven destroyed it with two shots. I winced, waiting for him to destroy me too, but the third shot didn't come. I looked up to see the Raven reload his rifle. Here was my chance! I sprinted the last few yards to the grenade, picked it up, then threw at my feet just as the Raven was aiming.

POW!

Back on the bus. I took a second to regain my composure, then marched to the back. That's right, I marched. No more limping. Sure, my leg still hurt, but now I was mad — mad at the Raven, mad at Vincenzo, mad at Mayor Parfait and his dumb money-making schemes. I was ready to win this thing.

That resolve lasted all of 30 seconds. I jumped out of the bus, landed in a farmhouse, looked out a window, and — wouldn't you know it — almost immediately spotted the Raven crossing a cornfield toward me.

Clomp, clomp, clomp.

I then heard someone walk noisily up the stairs on my left. I sighed and turned toward the door. "Let's get this over with."

The noise stopped. Then the person clomped back down the stairs.

"Wait!" I sprinted after the visitor. When I reached the bottom of the stairs, though, he was gone. Come on! I headed for the back door but slammed on the brakes just before I reached it. I'd never heard a door open. He was still in here. I ran around the first floor of the farmhouse with a Raven countdown clock ticking in my head. Finally, I found my visitor. One of those generic army guys was huddled underneath the stairs, clutching a rifle to his chest. One look at him told me he was a noob employing my old hide-and-seek strategy.

"It's OK, buddy!" I tried. "You can get your first kill, just…"

The noob shot wildly and spun past me toward the door.

"Hey! No, you don't!" I ran after him.

I dove and built a wall in front of the door just before he could reach it. "You're going to shoot me! And you're going to do it now!"

The noob turned around and fumbled with his gun. I waited patiently as he jumped and shot the ground a few times.

"You don't even have to jump, I'm not trying to shoot you."

Suddenly, the back door flew open. The Raven had arrived. I grabbed the noob by the shoulders to stop his dumb jumping. "DO IT NOW!"

BANG!

He did it.

I finally figured out what was going on during my third post-Jackson match. I landed in Tilted Towers to give myself plenty of cover, collected a sniper rifle, and perched on top of an apartment building. Sure enough, seconds later, the Raven rolled up to the edge of town. I ducked. The Raven looked around, then pulled a small tablet out of his suit. I zoomed in on the tablet with my sniper scope and saw that it showed a map of Tilted Towers with a red dot on my apartment building. The Raven took one look at the map, then started running toward my building.

I lowered the rifle. So he was tracking me. But how? As I thought about it, my leg started throbbing again, and suddenly I knew. That wasn't a bullet lodged in my leg. It was a tracker.

And that gave me an idea.

CHAPTER FIFTEEN

THE FINAL MATCH

OK, I understand that you might feel squeamish right now because you can see where this is headed. Everyone knows I could simply dig the tracker out of my leg, throw it across the room, and use it as bait to lure the Raven into an ambush. What could be easier?

Guess what? No way. No way, Jose. No way times a billion. If you think I'm going to perform minor surgery on myself with a pocket knife or something, you clearly have not been following along closely. No, I had another idea. It was not quite as bold as your gruesome theory (you sicko), but it could work for at least a little while.

When I caught a glimpse of the Raven's tracking system through my scope, I noticed that it was a flat map. That meant he couldn't know how high up in a building I might be. If I stuck to the apartment buildings and constantly stayed on the move, I just might be able to stay alive long enough to flip the odds on the Raven.

I looked at the sky and noticed it was starting to get dark. If my calculations were right, this was the last day of Vincenzo's fortnight. That would make this my final opportunity to win a match and return everything back to normal. I nodded to myself. Let's do this.

I hacked through the roof, grabbed a shotgun from the bedroom below, and…

BAM!

Took out some poor sap that happened to wander into the room at that moment. I reloaded, rounded the corner, and…

BAM!

Got my second kill. I glanced out a window in time to see the Raven enter my building. OK, I had about 30 seconds until he reached my level. I hacked through the floor, landed in the bathroom below and found a purple burst assault rifle.

Creak, creak, creak.

I paused when I heard someone walking up the stairs. I silently counted to three, spun around the corner, and took him out before he even saw me coming. My victim dropped a shield and a launchpad. I snatched everything while continuing to run. The timer in my head was ticking down — maybe 10 seconds left until the Raven arrived. I built ramps back up to the roof, equipped my shield, then dropped the launchpad on the corner of the rooftop. Before I used it, however, I noticed someone dressed as a skeleton running in the middle of the street. Three shots with my burst assault rifle, and he was gone. I grinned. Jackson wouldn't even be able to recognize me out here.

I jumped on the launchpad, equipped my glider, and floated to the tower across the street. To buy myself a few extra seconds, I circled around to a balcony in the back instead of the rooftop like the Raven would have expected. When I landed, I surprised a gingerbread woman who was aiming a rocket launcher out the window.

BAM!

I took her out with my shotgun, collected her weapon, then crouched at the window. This might be my one chance to surprise the Raven. I aimed at the rooftop I'd just left, and sure enough, the Raven appeared almost immediately. My palms got sweaty as I followed him with my rocket launcher. He jumped on the launchpad, then glided toward my building. I waited until I had the perfect shot, then…

ZING!

"AH!"

A sniper bullet hit me in the shoulder just as I squeezed the trigger. My rocket flew right past the Raven, alerting him and everyone else in the city where I was. I crouched as a half dozen more bullets flew through my window, then crawled across the room to hack an escape hole in the wall. I jumped out of the building just as the Raven entered it.

Machine gun bullets whizzed past my head as I sprinted across the street. I snatched grenades off the ground, then built a ramp to the second story of a bombed-out building. I climbed another level and waited with my heart beating through my chest for the Raven to run up my ramp so I could drop a grenade on him. But I didn't hear footsteps. I heard a different noise.

Chunk-chunk-chunk-chunk

I peeked outside to see three new forts in the middle of the street. Two guys wearing gas masks had intercepted the Raven as he chased me, and now all three of them were building and fighting at lightning speed. Soon, their forts were taller than any tower in the city. I silently thanked my new pals for buying me some time, then ran across town to put some distance between myself and the Raven. I climbed to the top of a tower, then pulled out my sniper scope to check out the action. I was just in time to see the Raven turn one of the gas mask guys to tar with his shotgun. The Raven then shifted his attention to the guy's unsuspecting buddy lower in the tower. I wanted to yell a warning, but I didn't have to.

BANG!

A surprise bullet hit the Raven in his shoulder. The Raven quickly built a protective roof over his head and disappeared inside his tower.

Where had that bullet come from? I quickly scanned the city. Nobody else could have possibly had the angle to hit the Raven like that; he was way too high. Wait a second... I looked up to the sky, and my jaw dropped. No. Way.

It was a skybase. Someone had somehow built a

skybase undetected over the busiest warzone on the whole island. I lifted my sniper rifle to take it out, but just before I pulled the trigger, I had a realization.

That skybase could save my life.

CHAPTER SIXTEEN
ENDGAME

If I could somehow reach the skybase, I could make myself appear to the Raven to be inside an apartment building even though I'd be standing 300 feet above it. I'd simply stand above a building, wait for the Raven to climb all the way to the top, then snipe him from the safety of my skybase. There was just one problem with my plan: the beginning. The bottom of the skybase ramp appeared to be hundreds of yards away. I'd never reach it before the Raven caught on.

I started pacing and glancing nervously at the Raven's fort. *CLUNK.* I looked down to see that I'd bumped into a shopping cart that someone had left on the roof. Who brings a shopping cart to a rooftop?

Waaaaiiiiiit a second.

I walked to the corner of the building that faced

away from the city, looked down, and smiled. A 100-foot drop. That could work. I pushed the cart to the edge of the building, took a deep breath, then ran off. The moment my feet left the ledge, I started building a ramp to the ground. I used my magical building power to call down wood from the sky faster and faster. Finally, when I reached the ground at a speed of 100 mph, I laid one more ramp to launch myself into the air.

ZOOM!

The shopping cart shot into the air like a bullet. While holding on to the cart with one hand, I used the other to fumble with the rocket launcher. I did my best to aim at the ground, then fired off a rocket.

ZOOOOOOM!

I went screaming toward the skybase ramp. I ducked to make myself more aerodynamic and tried not to close my eyes for the approach. Finally, the cart's front wheel *CLACK*ed against the ramp, flinging me upside down over the cart and almost over the ramp completely. I clawed the air as I flipped and somehow managed to grab the edge of the ramp. I hung there for a moment, glanced at the ground 150 feet down, and almost wet myself. I mustered enough strength to pull myself up and lay panting on the ramp. After a few moments, I brushed myself off and snuck up the ramp.

The skybase's builder was a generic army guy, which — I was now realizing — was the costume of a noob. That knowledge gave me the courage to creep up to him. I could shoot him if I needed to, but my goal was to get rid of him silently so no one else would think to look up. I crept for what felt like an eternity until I was right behind him. Then, I pushed him off the ramp.

"AHHHHHhhhhh!"

I smiled at my good luck when I leaned over the edge to watch his fall. Not only was the noob easy to take out, but he'd also built directly over an apartment building! Judging by the launchpad in the corner of the roof, it was the very building I'd landed on to start the game. My Raven trap was already set! I rubbed my hands together and checked my watch. Four people left in the game. That meant me, two other players, and the Raven. And oh, look! More good luck. One of the two contestants had just arrived on top of the apartment roof to check out the noise. That meant the Raven would take him out so I wouldn't have to. I pulled out my sniper rifle to get a better look at the poor sap. It was getting dark, but through my scope, I should be able to…

Oh no.

I lowered my scope. It was Jackson.

I'd reunited with my best friend at the worst possible time. The Raven had the element of surprise and would absolutely take Jackson out the second he arrived on the roof. A quick scan of the city confirmed my worst fear — the Raven had just entered Jackson's building. I had 30 seconds.

What could I do? Jackson couldn't hear me down there. If I tried firing a warning shot, he'd just destroy my skybase before realizing it was me.

Twenty-five seconds.

If I abandoned the skybase, I couldn't guarantee that the Raven would leave Jackson's building before reaching the top.

Twenty seconds.

If I killed Jackson to save him from the Raven, the other player in the game would easily find my skybase and kill me before I could win the game.

Fifteen seconds.

I clenched my jaw and steadied my breathing. I knew what I had to do. I trained my sniper rifle on the hole in the roof right behind Jackson. I had to kill the Raven before he could take out my best friend.

Ten seconds.

I'd only have time for one shot.

Nine seconds.

I drew a deep breath, then slowly let it out.

Eight seconds.

I could do this. I had to do this.

Seven seconds.

But before I got my chance…

CRACK!

The skybase crumbled underneath my feet. I flailed and panicked as I tumbled through the air. What happened?!

Six seconds.

Then I saw it. A Viking dancing on top of a fort across the street. The third player in this little game had finally spotted my skybase and gleefully destroyed it.

Five seconds.

"Jackson!" I screamed. "JAAAAAAACKSON!" He couldn't hear me. Even worse, he was walking back toward the hole in the roof.

Four seconds.

I desperately dug through my backpack for something that could stop the inevitable. Pickax? No. Rifle? No. Wood bundle? No.

Three seconds.

My hand brushed against something small and metal. A grenade.

Two seconds.

Out of options and out of hope, I chucked the grenade as hard as I could toward the hole in the roof.

One second.

The Raven's head popped up right in front of

Jackson. Jackson recoiled as the Raven pulled out his gun.

BOOM!

My grenade exploded right between Jackson and the Raven, swallowing both of them in a white flash.

I breathed a sigh of relief and turned to watch the Viking celebrate victory as I plummeted to my death. Sure, I was seconds away from losing both this game and Vincenzo's challenge, but I'd saved my best friend, and that's all that mattered. I couldn't help but cringe a little as I prepared to hit the roof. I squeezed my eyes shut and curled into a ball, but the roof never came. I hit something else instead.

BOING!

I sprang back in the air and spun around to see that I'd landed directly on the launchpad I'd set back at the beginning of the game. Wait a second, if I hit the launchpad, that meant I could deploy my glider!

SHING!

I grinned and turned toward the dancing Viking. I didn't exactly have a plan at the moment, but surely I'd think of something along the way, right?

Surely not.

I grew more and more frustrated with myself the closer I got to the Viking. Here was a prime opportunity to take out someone dancing like he'd won the game, and my mind was blank. When I reached the fort, I just decided to wing it and ended up pulling the lamest move possible: I flailed my legs like an idiot.

Guess what? It worked.

I ended up kicking the Viking square in the chest. He didn't even see it coming because he was spinning with his eyes closed and happy hands in the air. The kick pushed him off the edge of the fort, but not before he grabbed my leg. We spun and tumbled to the ground, him trying to claw at my glider, and me trying to remove his pointy Viking helmet from my stomach. Finally…

WHAM!

We crashed to the ground.

CHAPTER SEVENTEEN

ONE MORE GAME

KNOCK! KNOCK! KNOCK!

I opened my eyes. For the first time in weeks, I found myself staring at my bedroom ceiling instead of the back of a grimy bus seat.

KNOCK! KNOCK! KNOCK!

"Coming!" I tried to yell. Instead, I mumbled, "Blumbing." As soon as I rolled out of bed, I crumpled to the ground. All the running and jumping I'd done during the battle royale had finally caught up with me — my legs felt like jelly. I clutched the bed, got back up, and wobbled down the stairs. As I stumbled, I started to hear a chant outside. "PETE! PETE! PETE! PETE!" When I finally opened the door, I was greeted by a loud cheer from half the residents of the island and

Mayor Parfait. That cheer quickly quieted to awkward silence once everyone got a look at me.

"Hi," I said. More silence. Then I felt a breeze on my legs and realized why everyone had gone silent. I was again not wearing any pants.

"Ahem, uh, hello, Pants, I mean Pete," Mayor Parfait said as he tried super hard not to look at my boxers. "I am here to congratulate you on behalf of the residents of Perfect Potty Island for winning the battle royale and returning us back to our way of life. You are a true legend."

I shifted uncomfortably and avoided eye contact with the mayor. "No problem."

"Please accept this trophy for your victory." Mayor Parfait held out a dainty umbrella.

"Uh, wow, thanks," I said as I grabbed the umbrella. The crowd gave a weak cheer. Mayor Parfait stared for a second like he wanted me to give a speech or something, but I didn't open my mouth. I finally nodded, which prompted Mayor Parfait to turn to the crowd, declare the whole operation a success, and encourage everyone to give me space to put on pants.

As the crowd started walking away, I heard a familiar voice. "Pete!"

I grinned when I saw Jackson. "Sorry for blowing you up back there."

Jackson finally got through the crowd and did a complicated handshake with me. "You were unbelievable!"

I waved him off and walked back into the house. "Just trying to be like you."

"But how did you do it?" Jackson asked as he followed me up the stairs, unfazed by my boxers. "I mean there was another guy, right?"

I pulled on a pair of sweatpants when I reached my bedroom. "It was the dumbest thing. I…"

RIIIIIIING!

My sentence got cut off by the phone on my nightstand. I glanced over and felt a familiar panic in the pit of my stomach. The screen had inexplicably turned purple.

RIIIIIIING!

I looked at Jackson. I could tell he was thinking the same thing I was.

RIIIIIIING!

"Get rid of it," Jackson whispered. "Just throw it out the window."

I wanted to get rid of it. I wanted to so much. I just couldn't bring myself to touch it. Jackson and I stared at the phone, waiting for it to ring again. But it never did. Instead, the sound of slow breathing came from the speakers. After a few moments of creepy breathing, Vincenzo's voice wheezed, "Congratulations."

I held my breath.

After some more slow breathing, Vincenzo finally asked, "One more game?"

"No," I said, trying to make myself sound tough. "I won fair and square."

Silence. Long, uninterrupted silence. I had to lean into the phone to make sure Vincenzo was still there. "Did you hear me?" I asked, gaining a little confidence. "We're done."

DING.

I nearly jumped out of my skin when my phone dinged to let me know I had a message. Without waiting for me to touch the screen, the message opened itself and started playing a video. In the video, a man covered in black tar was strapped to the hospital gurney in Vincenzo's hideout. I watched in stunned silence as he pleaded for his life.

Jackson covered his mouth. "Is that…"

I nodded. It was Dale. Our mailman.

After the video finished, Vincenzo's wheezing laugh started up again. "One more game," he repeated.

This time, it wasn't a question.

A NOTE FROM THE AUTHOR

Thanks for reading my book! Hope you liked it. If you did, why not review it on Amazon? If you didn't, maybe keep it to yourself.

You can stay up-to-date on when the next Battle Island book is coming out by signing up at MattKorver.com. You can also send me a message any time at matt@mattkorver.com.

Made in the USA
Middletown, DE
18 July 2020

13122446R00076